ADVENTURES at TABBY TOWERS

Raintree is an imprint of Capstone Global Library Limited, a company incorporated in England and Wales having its registered office at 264 Banbury Road, Oxford, OX2 7DY – Registered company number: 6695582

www.raintree.co.uk
myorders@raintree.co.uk

Edited by Jill Kalz
Designed by Heidi Thompson
Original illustrations @ Capstone Global Library LImited 2018
Illustrated by Deborah Melmon
Production by Kathy McColley
Originated by Capstone Global Library
Printed and bound in China.

ISBN 978 1 474 74880 3
21 20 19 18 17
10 9 8 7 6 5 4 3 2 1

British Library Cataloguing in Publication Data
A full catalogue record for this book is available from the British Library.

Leaping Lizzie

by Shelley Swanson Sateren
illustrated by Deborah Melmon

CONTENTS

ADVENTURES at TABBY TOWERS

IT'S TIME FOR YOUR ADVENTURE AT TABBY TOWERS!

At Tabby Towers, we give cats the royal treatment. We are a first-class cats-only hotel that promises a safe, fun stay for all guests.

Tabby Towers has many cat toys and games. We make personal play time for every guest. And we have a large indoor kitty playground that will satisfy every cat instinct, including climbing and hunting. Also, your kitty will never tire of watching our cow and chickens from the big playground window.

We are always just a short walk away from the cats. Tabby Towers is located in a large, sunny, heated room at the back of our farmhouse. Every cat has a private litter box and a private, three-level "apartment", complete with bed, toys and dishes. Of course, we will follow your feeding schedule too.

TABBY TOWERS WHO'S WHO

KIT FELINUS

Kit Felinus (fee-LEE-nus) is a lifelong cat lover. She has worked for cat rescue and shelter operations much of her adult life. After seeing the great success of Hound Hotel – the dog hotel next door – she realized the need for a cat hotel in the area. So she started Tabby Towers. She now cares for cats all day long and couldn't be happier!

TOM FELINUS

Tom Felinus is certain that his wife, Kit, fell in love with him because of his last name, which means "cat-like". He is a retired builder. He built Tabby Towers' kitty apartments, cat trees and scratching posts. He built the playground equipment too, which will keep your kitty happy for hours.

TABITHA CATARINA FELINUS (TABBY CAT, FOR SHORT)

Tabby Cat is Kit and Tom's granddaughter and a true cat lover. In fact, the cat hotel is named after her! She helps at Tabby Towers in summer. The 8-year-old daughter of two vets, Tabby lives in the city and has her own cat. She's read almost as many books about cats as her grandma has! Tabby will give your kitty all the extra attention or playtime he or she may need.

Next time your family goes on holiday, bring your cat to Tabby Towers.

Your kitty is sure to have a purr-fect time!

CHAPTER 1
Queen Lizzie arrives

I'm Tabitha Catarina – Tabby Cat, for short. I L-O-V-E, love cats. I've loved them my whole life. I even have a cat of my own – a beautiful Himalayan cat called Bootsie.

Last spring, I had three choices for where to spend the upcoming summer.

Choice Number One: on a film set with my parents. They're both vets. They take care of animals that appear in films. That's their job.

I said, “No, thank you” because there weren’t going to be any cat actors – only horses.

Choice Number Two: in the city, at our apartment, with my nanny, Pam. She was going to house-sit for the summer.

Choice Number Three: on my grandparents’ farm, where they run their amazing cat hotel, Tabby Towers.

Can you guess what my choice was?

Yes, I’m here at Tabby Towers. I feel like the luckiest girl alive. I get to play with cats seven days a week. I get to help care for them. And I get to spend time with Grandma Kit and Grandpa Tom.

So far, this has been my best summer ever.

But there’s a problem. The problem is a girl my age called Alfreeda Wolfe. She lives on the farm next door to my grandparents’ place.

Her family runs a dog hotel.

I'd like to be better friends with her, but she always brags about dogs and puts down cats. It makes me *so* cross. She even said mean things about a famous cat called Lizzie, while Lizzie was a guest at Tabby Towers last month.

Do you think I started to hiss at Alfreeda? Well, here's what happened.

🐾 🐾 🐾

It was an early afternoon at the beginning of July. Grandma Kit and I were busy working in the cat hotel.

Tabby Towers is on the main floor of my grandparents' farmhouse. It used to be their family room.

Grandpa Tom built everything for the hotel: the cat trees, scratching posts and seven kitty apartments, where the guests sleep at night.

Grandma Kit was cleaning dishes in the sink. I was playing a string game with a guest called Puppycat. He was a large Maine coon. Maine coons need a lot of exercise every day, and I made sure Puppycat got his.

Two cute kittens – Fifi and her brother, Furbaby – chased each other around the indoor kitty playground. They zoomed around and around like two furry racing cars.

Then Furbaby shot up a tall ladder, and Fifi followed. They ran along a narrow catwalk near the ceiling. Grandpa Tom built that too. I call it the "kitty highway".

Another guest – Child – sat on a shelf, high in a cat tree. Child was a Persian, with long, fluffy hair. He licked his legs and paws. Like most cats, Child spent a lot of time cleaning himself each day.

I saw Grandpa Tom out the big window that overlooked the farmyard. He was fixing a fence between our land and the Wolfes' farm. He'd probably be out there until dinner time.

Anyway, the doorbell rang, and Puppycat and I jumped.

"Now who could that be?" Grandma Kit asked, wiping a large tray with a soapy cloth. "I'm not expecting any new guests to check in this afternoon."

"I'll go and see who it is," I offered.

"Thanks," Grandma Kit said. "I'll wash my hands and be there in a minute."

I set Puppycat on a kitty swing, gave it a gentle push and then hurried to the front door. Before I opened it, I peeked out the window.

A pizza-company truck was parked in the driveway. Large letters on the side said: QUEEN LIZZIE'S PIZZA PALACE.

That's the new pizza place in town, I thought. *Today's their grand opening!*

A big picture of a strange-looking cat was printed above the letters. That was Queen Lizzie. I'd seen her picture lots of times in the town newspaper. The restaurant had placed a lot of adverts lately.

The man standing on our porch looked around nervously. I'd seen his picture in the newspaper too. His name was Ben, and he was the pizza restaurant's owner. He was holding a cat carrier.

"Hi!" I said, throwing open the front door. I pointed at the carrier. "Is that Queen Lizzie? *The* Queen Lizzie?"

Ben nodded. He looked a bit sad.

"I can't believe you brought her to Tabby Towers!" I cried. "Come in!"

CHAPTER 2
Hairless with huge ears

I was so excited to meet Queen Lizzie, I couldn't stop talking.

"A real Sphynx cat! Wow. I know she's a Sphynx cat because I've read so much about them," I said. "I know lots of people think Sphynx look strange because they're hairless and have those huge ears and extra-large paws. Well, I don't think Sphynx are strange. Personally, I think they are terribly interesting. I've never seen one in real life!"

I kneeled and peered into the cat carrier.

"Hi, Lizzie! I'm Tabby. I love your yellow eyes," I exclaimed. "They look like lemons!"

Just then, Grandma Kit appeared at my side, drying her hands. She said hello to Ben and shook his hand.

"I'm Ben, the owner of the new pizza shop in town," he said. "This is Lizzie, the restaurant's namesake. I've come to you for help."

Grandma Kit didn't even have a chance to reply. I'd barely taken a breath but carried right on, chattering about Lizzie.

"I love her high cheekbones," I said. "And her pink skin is so cool. Look at those grey spots. It's like she's got polka-dots! I read in one of my cat books that the colour of a Sphynx's skin is the colour its hair would be."

"That's true," Ben said. His voice matched his unhappy-looking face.

Strange, I thought. *How can anyone be sad when they own such a special cat?*

"I also read that Sphynx are great climbers and jumpers," I went on.

"That's part of the problem," Ben said.

"Why don't you come into the kitchen," Grandma Kit said. "I'll make tea, then you can tell us what's going on with Lizzie."

Ben agreed and followed us inside. He sat at the kitchen table. I sat on the floor beside Lizzie's carrier.

I wanted to reach inside and touch her hairless, wrinkled skin. But I didn't. Instead, I talked to her in a soft, quiet voice. It's always important that first meetings with cats go slowly and peacefully.

Grandma Kit made tea, while Ben told us the problem.

"As you know, today is the restaurant's grand opening," he said. "I should be there right now. The place is packed with pizza lovers. Business is booming already. But Lizzie kept jumping up onto the front desk and worktops. And we can't have her that close to the food. There are special health codes we need to follow."

"Oh dear," Grandma Kit said. She poured tea into a cup for Ben.

He took a sip and continued. "I'd really hoped Lizzie would stay in the front window for people to see. She's such a friendly cat.

I was certain she'd let people pet her, even strangers. She has before, at my apartment, anyhow. It would've been good for business."

Grandma Kit nodded and took a sip of tea. "Go on," she said.

"Even the town leaders said Lizzie could stay in the restaurant," he said. "Because she's hairless, she's cleaner. I put her bed and toys in the front window. But during the very first lunch rush, she kept jumping onto the surfaces. I'd say 'no' and put her back in the window. She'd jump right back onto the front desk again. Boxes of pizza sit right there."

"Is she hungry for pizza?" I asked.

"No," Ben said. "I've offered bits of crust to her before. She doesn't like it. I even sprayed her with water, to scare her off the worktop. That didn't work."

“Well, cats *do* like to climb to high places and lie on top of things,” I said.

“I know,” Ben said. “But she can’t be on the restaurant’s front desk. That’s too near the food.” He looked at Grandma Kit. “It’s short notice, but could Lizzie check in here at Tabby Towers? I’ll be working long hours all week.”

“Why, yes,” Grandma Kit said with a smile. “It would be our pleasure. We have space in the hotel. But it’s a shame the restaurant’s namesake can’t be there during your big opening week.”

Ben nodded. “Thank you very much. The staff and I will really miss her,” he said.

I felt bad for Ben – but secretly happy for me. I couldn’t believe a Sphynx would be staying at Tabby Towers! Wow! I really *was* the luckiest girl alive!

“Can I take her out of her carrier?” I asked Ben. “Would she let me hold her?”

“Sure,” he said. “Go ahead. Lizzie loves to be held.”

I carefully opened the carrier door. “Here, girl,” I said quietly. “Come here, Lizzie.”

Lizzie crawled right into my arms. I sat and cradled her, rubbing her soft skin gently with my hand. Her skin was covered with very fine down, like the skin of a peach.

Suddenly the kitchen door flew open. *Bang*!

“Hey, did you order pizza?” a girl called, bursting into the room. It was Alfreeda Wolfe, the dog-loving girl from next door.

The second the door banged, Lizzie leaped out of my arms. She sprang up – a shockingly high leap – and landed right on top of the refrigerator, bumping into a cat-shaped treat jar. The glass jar flew off the refrigerator and fell to the floor.

"Oh no!" cried Ben.

CHAPTER 3

One crazy cat

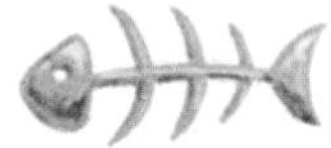

Crash! The treat jar hit the floor and broke into pieces. Chunks of glass lay among cat treats that had filled the jar. The treats belonged to Scruffy, Grandma Kit's cat.

Good thing Scruffy is outside right now, I thought with a shiver. *If he were inside, he'd jump into that dangerous mess to get those treats.*

"That's one crazy cat," Alfreeda said. She pointed at Lizzie, who was still on top of the refrigerator. "She's jumping to such high places, knocking down breakable stuff. . . . What a mess. A dog would never do that. A dog would be better behaved."

I frowned at her.

Grandma Kit raised an eyebrow at me. It was the look she often gave me when Alfreeda was around. It meant this: *Tabitha, be nice. We're neighbours.*

I kept my mouth shut. But I really wanted to shout at Alfreeda, *Can't you see* you *caused this mess?*

Lizzie sat perfectly still, except for her tail. It hung over the edge of the refrigerator and wagged. That wasn't a good sign. In the dog world, a wagging tail means happiness or excitement. In the cat world, a low-hanging, wagging tail means the cat is upset.

Grandma Kit started sweeping up the mess.

"I'm so sorry, Kit," Ben said.

"No problem at all," she said, placing glass pieces and cat treats into the rubbish bin.

"I'll be more than happy to pay for the treat jar," Ben offered.

"No need," Grandma Kit said. "I have five more cat-shaped treat jars in the basement. People always give me cat-lover gifts."

Alfreeda looked at the table. "So, no pizza?" she asked.

"Sorry, we didn't order any," Grandma Kit said. "Queen Lizzie has come to stay at Tabby Towers for a while."

"What? The hairless cat from the newspaper ads?" Alfreeda asked, her eyes growing to twice their usual size. "That's her? Queen Lizzie? *The* Queen Lizzie? Wow, she looks even stranger in real life. How is her strangeness supposed to make people want to eat pizza?"

Grandma Kit cleared her throat. "Alfreeda?" she said. "This is Ben, the owner of Queen Lizzie's Pizza Palace."

"Oh. Hi, Ben," Alfreeda said. She shut her mouth but opened it right up again. "What were you thinking, showing a wrinkled, hairless cat in your ads? Maybe you could adopt a cool dog, call it Lizzie and put *her* in the ads."

Ben sighed. "No," he said. "Lizzie's my girl. She's more than a princess to me. She's a queen. Queen Lizzie. We just have a little problem with her, that's all. She won't stay off the restaurant's front desk."

"Of course, she won't," Alfreeda said. "Unlike dogs, cats can't be trained to obey rules. It's hopeless. Simply hopeless."

Ben sighed again and turned to Grandma Kit. "Thank you for your help," he said. "I'll be in touch when things calm down at the restaurant. Oh, I forgot to bring Lizzie's food. I'm sure she's hungry too. She didn't eat a bite all morning."

"Don't worry," Grandma Kit said. "We have plenty of cat food. I'll see you out." She led Ben towards the front door.

Well, I was getting crosser with Alfreeda by the second. I wanted to prove that cats could be trained – to prove her wrong *and* to make Ben happy.

I remembered something I'd read about cats jumping onto kitchen surfaces. It was in one of my cat books. It had suggested a few possible ways to fix the problem.

"Wait, Ben!" I cried, leaping cat-like into the living room.

CHAPTER 4

Pink-and-grey rocket

I caught Ben just as he got to the door. He stopped and turned.

"I think I can fix the problem," I said. "I've just remembered – one of my cat books has good tips for keeping cats off kitchen surfaces."

"Really?" said Ben. "Well, if you can fix this, I'll give you free pizza for a month. Deal?"

"Deal," I said, shaking his hand.

"Tabitha, please take Lizzie to the hotel," Grandma Kit said. "Get her settled in a bit.

Ben has her vet papers in his truck. I'll walk him out and get them. I'll be back in a minute."

First I ran up to my room and grabbed the cat book I needed. Then I hurried to the kitchen and placed a chair next to the refrigerator. I climbed onto it and gathered Lizzie in my arms. She snuggled into my chest. I carried her to the back of the house.

Alfreeda had been looking at framed photos of cats on the kitchen wall. Now she marched right behind me, without even asking if she could visit the hotel. There was nothing new about that. She always followed me around like an annoying puppy. She usually chose the moments when I most wanted to be alone too.

The other four guests – Fifi, Furbaby, Puppycat and Child – were in their kitty apartments. Seven kitty apartments lined the wall in the large, sun-filled room.

Each small apartment was three levels with a screen door. Every cat had its own safe, cozy, private space. Grandma Kit had put the guests inside their apartments before meeting Ben. We never leave the kitties outside their apartments if we're not there to watch them.

"Do you want to know why I came over?" Alfreeda asked.

No, I thought.

"It wasn't the pizza truck," Alfreeda continued. "It was to see if you wanted to eat dinner at my house tonight. I mean, here it is, July. We've hardly hung out at all. There aren't any other girls my age around. I need a break from my brother. He can be *so* annoying."

I know what that's like, I thought.

"Come on, Tabby Cat. Dinner. My place. Want to?" she asked.

"Thanks," I said. "We'll see. I want to try training Lizzie first."

Alfreeda threw a toy mouse in the air, caught it and threw it up again. "Don't bother," she said. "It's a waste of time trying to train a cat."

I felt the hair rise on top of my head. *Be nice, be nice,* I told myself.

I took a deep breath and carried Lizzie to the worktop by the sink. I put her on the floor, facing the worktop. Grandma Kit always filled the cat-food dishes on that worktop. I opened the cat book and skimmed the training tips.

"We'll practise here, Lizzie," I said in a gentle, quiet voice. "I'm going to teach you to stay off this worktop – and *all* worktops, okay? But first, you have to get *on* it. Then I'll teach you to get *off* it." I patted the worktop. "Here, girl. Come, girl. Jump up, Lizzie."

She didn't move.

Alfreeda laughed – loudly.

In a blink, Lizzie jumped. She shot like a pink-and-grey rocket into the air. She landed halfway up a cat tree, on top of a small shelf.

"Wow!" Alfreeda cried. "Did you see how high she jumped?"

I shrugged. "Yeah. Cats jump like that all the time. No big deal. You mean, *dogs* can't jump five times their height?"

Alfreeda didn't say anything.

Ha, I thought. *Got her there.*

Alfreeda and I watched Lizzie jump from the cat tree to a kitty ladder on the side wall. She climbed it easily, then leaped to a narrow beam close to the ceiling. It was the highest perch in the whole playground.

Lizzie lay on the beam and stared out of the big window at the farmyard. Her tail hung down and wagged. She was bothered by something. No doubt the "something" was Alfreeda's big, loud mouth.

"Queen Lizzie must have strong back legs," Alfreeda said.

“Actually, all cats do,” I said. “Sphynx have extra-powerful ones.”

“Not as powerful as a dog’s,” Alfreeda argued.

“More powerful than a *small* dog’s,” I said.

Alfreeda didn’t say anything.

Ha again, I thought.

I found a can of tuna in the cupboard and emptied it into a kitty dish. The room filled with the strong smell of fish.

I put the dish on the worktop. “Lizzie will smell it and jump onto the worktop,” I said. “Then we’ll start training. Watch, she’ll come right down. Cats have a powerful sense of smell, stronger than a person’s.”

“Not as powerful as a dog’s,” Alfreeda argued.

My fingers curled into fists. The hair rose at the back of my neck. Alfreeda was such a pain!

She was driving me *crazy*! I bit my tongue to stop myself shouting at her.

I spun around and took another can of tuna from the cupboard. I emptied it into the dish. Now the room smelled twice as fishy.

"Come, Lizzie," I called. "Come and get the tasty tuna, girl."

Alfreeda laughed again. "Unlike dogs, cats don't come when you call. Cats do *not* obey people. Cats *can't* be trained. Okay?"

"*Not* okay!" I snapped. "You're *wrong*!"

"Whoa," Alfreeda said, backing away. "Someone's acting catty."

I frowned at her. "Look, I have ideas that will fix Lizzie's problem. I *will* train her to stay off worktops. I *will* earn a month of free pizza. I'll earn it by dinner time today! Just watch me!"

Alfreeda rolled her eyes.

"I need to get some supplies," I said. I gave my head a proud shake and flipped my ponytail as I walked out the door.

I'd show Alfreeda!

CHAPTER 5
Hundreds of places to hide

Ten minutes later, I carried a basket filled with supplies to the hotel door. I knocked.

"All clear?" I called.

"All clear," Grandma Kit called back.

"All clear" meant no cats or kittens crept near the door, ready to spring past my feet.

"Watch your step," Grandma Kit added. "Child's out of his apartment now."

I opened the door and headed inside. I quickly realized I couldn't "watch my step".

I couldn't see around the big basket in my arms. It held a baking tray, a bottle of salad oil, a bottle of dish soap, a picnic-table cloth, a roll of double-sided tape and a bag of balloons.

Suddenly Grandma Kit cried, "Look out, Tabitha! Don't step –"

Too late. My shoe landed on something wet. My foot slid forwards. My legs flew in front of me. The basket shot into the air.

I fell to the floor and landed, full force, on my left hand. "Ow!" I shouted. Pain shot up my wrist and into my arm.

That same second, the baking tray fell to the floor with a *bang*! The oil bottle hit the floor with a *thud*! The soap bottle did too.

Groaning, I lay on my back and watched Lizzie's actions after the loud noises. She leaped from the beam to the top of a cat tree. Then she darted around and around the narrow kitty highway near the ceiling.

"Are you okay?" Alfreeda asked me.

I couldn't believe Alfreeda was still here.

"I think so," I said.

"You stepped on a hairball," Grandma Kit explained. "Child just threw it up. I'll get the mop and bucket from the basement."

"Gross," Alfreeda said, wrinkling her nose. "That hairball stinks. Good thing dogs don't get them."

"Dogs throw up sometimes," I argued. "I bet they throw up lots of nasty stuff."

"Whatever," Alfreeda said with a shrug.

Grandma Kit opened the basement door just as I tried to sit up. A sharp pain shot through my wrist again.

"I think I've sprained my wrist," I said.

Grandma Kit kneeled beside me and gently rubbed my wrist.

"Ow!" I cried.

"It's not broken," she said. "But it does seem to be sprained. Wait here."

A few minutes later, I was still sitting next to the stinky hairball. Grandma Kit got a bag of frozen peas from the freezer.

"That's a good thing about hairless cats, like Lizzie," she said. "They don't get hairballs. Their tummies don't fill with fur when they clean themselves with their tongues."

Alfreeda picked up all the things that had flown out of the basket. She placed them on the worktop. "What's this stuff for?" she asked.

"Supplies for training Lizzie to stay off worktops," I said. "Most cats don't like wet, sticky stuff on their paws. I think Grandma Kit would say no to some of my ideas, so I brought a lot of supplies."

"Let's hear your ideas," Grandma Kit said.

"Okay. My first idea is to cover the worktop with salad oil," I said. "What do you think?

Lizzie would jump onto the worktop and slide around. She wouldn't like that feeling at all. She'd never go on the worktop again."

"No. Too messy," Grandma Kit said. "I don't want oily paw prints all over Tabby Towers."

"Okay, then, I'll cover the worktop with a picnic-table cloth," I said. "And I'll put soapy water on the cloth. Just a little. It's the same idea – Lizzie won't like the feeling of her paws sliding around."

"Too unsafe," Grandma Kit said. "She might slide off the worktop and get hurt. What are your other ideas?"

"I could fill the bottom of the tray with water," I said. "She wouldn't like the wetness. Or I could cover the worktop with double-sided tape. She wouldn't like the stickiness. Or I could blow up balloons and tape them to the worktop. Her sharp claws would pop them.

The noise would scare her, and she'd never go on any worktops again."

"Those ideas just might work. Clever girl," Grandma Kit said. "Now rest this bag of frozen peas on your wrist. The cold will help keep down the swelling."

She pressed on the bag just a bit, and pain travelled up my arm.

"Ow!" I shouted.

Lizzie jumped. She leaped from the kitty-cat highway all the way to the floor.

"Wow! Did you see *that*?" Alfreeda cried.

Lizzie darted across the playground floor in a flash of pink and grey. She tore through the open basement door and down the steps.

"Oh no," Grandma Kit groaned. "We'll never find her down there. The basement is huge.

It's packed with a lifetime of belongings. There are hundreds of places to hide."

She jumped up and ran down the basement steps. "Lizzie! Come, Lizzie!"

Alfreeda and I ran after Grandma Kit.

Poor, scared Lizzie, I thought. *We have to find her and help calm her down.*

CHAPTER 6
A+ for climbing skills

Grandma Kit was right about one thing: The basement was packed with belongings. A lifetime of cat-lover gifts filled the shelves. There were stuffed toy kitties, framed cat pictures, cat-shaped cookie jars, leopard-print blankets, tiger-stripe handbags and much, much more.

But Grandma Kit was wrong about one thing too: Lizzie wasn't hard to find.

The cat sat on top of a narrow pipe near the ceiling, the highest perch in the basement.

Parts of the pipe were wrapped in cloth, so Lizzie could hang on easily. Her claws dug into the wrapping.

"She gets an A+ for climbing skills," I said. "She must've jumped to the pipe from the top of the boiler. Then she climbed across that skinny pipe. I'm impressed."

The big, old boiler heated the big, old farmhouse in the wintertime. The boiler had eight thick pipes sticking out of its wide, round belly. It looked like a giant octopus.

"It's just like a cat to climb to a super-high place and make people save her," Alfreeda said. "Dogs don't have to be saved from tall trees or rooftops or ceiling pipes."

My jaw tightened and I ground my teeth.

Grandma Kit gave me "the look" and a slow, warning headshake. I kept my mouth shut.

But I truly didn't know how much more of Alfreeda Wolfe I could stand that afternoon.

"I'll get Lizzie down," Alfreeda said.

"No, *I* will," I snapped.

I stepped onto the boiler's door handle. I reached up with both hands and grabbed an octopus arm. I tried to pull myself up. The worst pain yet shot through my wrist. "Ow!" I said and jumped down. "I guess I can't do it, after all."

"I can't climb either," Grandma Kit said, patting her leg. "I hurt my knee a couple of days ago."

"So, I'll do it," Alfreeda offered again.

"No," I snapped. "Lizzie doesn't need your help. Cats can get down from high places by themselves. People just need to give them enough time, that's all."

"But I want Lizzie back upstairs now, Tabitha," Grandma Kit said. "It's my job to keep her safe. There are too many sharp tools and breakable things down here."

"Okay, then," Alfreeda said with a grin. "Here I go. Alfreeda the Amazing Kitty-Cat Saver to the rescue!"

I frowned. Grandma Kit looked at me and put her finger to her lips.

"Fine," I said quietly.

Quick as a cat, Alfreeda climbed up the boiler and stood on top of it. She reached up and took hold of Lizzie's pipe with both hands. Hand-over-hand, she moved across the pipe towards Lizzie. Her legs swung above big boxes and cat-print suitcases.

Soon she'd be within a metre of Lizzie. "Almost there!" Alfreeda shouted.

Lizzie jumped and nearly fell. Grandma Kit gasped. I slapped my good hand over my mouth. My heart beat quickly.

"Oops," Alfreeda whispered. "Sorry. Forgot about loud noises. I better be quieter."

No kidding, I thought.

Lizzie quickly caught her balance and darted further down the narrow pipe. She stopped and sat down again.

"Show me a *dog* with such excellent balance," I said.

"Shhh," Alfreeda whispered.

Hand-over-hand, Alfreeda moved across the pipe until she hung just below Lizzie. Then she reached up with one hand and lifted Lizzie by the tummy. She put the cat on her shoulder.

"Hang on, girl," Alfreeda said in a soft voice.

Lizzie must've dug her claws into Alfreeda's shoulder because Alfreeda's face wrinkled in pain. "Ow," she whispered.

With both hands back on the pipe, Alfreeda moved towards the boiler. She dropped onto it, then jumped to the floor, with Lizzie safely on her shoulder.

"Good job," I said. And I actually meant it.

"Thanks," Alfreeda said, smiling.

Once we got upstairs again, we made sure the basement door was shut tight. We put Lizzie inside her cozy apartment for some quiet time. I gave her the tuna, and she gobbled it right up.

"I'm hungry too," said Alfreeda.

"I could eat *ten* cans of tuna," I said.

"How about pizza at the new restaurant in town?" Grandma Kit asked, patting Alfreeda on the back. "My treat, for saving Lizzie."

"Excellent." Alfreeda grinned. "I get to have dinner with Tabby Cat, after all."

CHAPTER 7
Changing the subject

Before long, Grandma Kit, Grandpa Tom, Alfreeda and I were sitting at a table at Queen Lizzie's Pizza Palace. We sipped lemonade and waited for the onion and extra-cheese pizza we'd ordered.

A large picture of Lizzie hung on the far wall. She wore a crown. The picture had a fancy frame around it.

The restaurant looked like the dining hall in a castle. Wooden beams crossed the high ceiling. Big tables filled the large room.

The waiters dressed like people from the Middle Ages. They looked really cool. I even saw two knights in shining armour!

A wood-fired oven filled the wall behind the front desk. Piles of firewood were stacked next to it. Chefs put pizza after pizza into the oven to bake.

The place was packed with pizza lovers. The busy waiters leaped, cat-like, between tables, bringing food and drinks.

More hungry people arrived. The headwaiter rang a bell and shouted "Welcome!" every time a guest entered the restaurant.

I watched people eating pizza, and my mouth watered. I couldn't wait!

But I *had* to wait. And I had to listen to Alfreeda chatter on and on about dogs too. Grandma Kit tried to change the subject.

She even thanked Alfreeda again for saving Lizzie in the basement.

"No problem," Alfreeda said. "But that's a cat for you. A dog would never run into a room and look for the highest spot to hang out."

That did it. I snapped, "Would you *please* stop bragging about dogs and putting down –"

Grandma Kit kicked me under the table.

I shut my mouth. I spun sideways in my seat so I wouldn't have to look at Alfreeda anymore. I frowned at the front desk that had started this problem in the first place.

Then I looked around the rest of the restaurant. And I slowly began to realize something – something important.

Suddenly I sat up straight, snapped my fingers and cried, "That's it!"

CHAPTER 8
Kitty castle in the clouds

I spun back around in my seat to face Alfreeda and my grandparents.

"That's *what,* Tabitha?" Grandma Kit asked.

I pointed across the restaurant. "See Lizzie's bed in the front window?" I said. "It's right by the very busy front door, by that loud bell. I bet Lizzie feels really unsafe with all the noise and strangers."

"Ah! You're thinking like a cat," Grandpa Tom said with a grin. "Go on."

"Now, look at the front desk," I continued. "It's the highest flat space in the whole restaurant – the highest perch a scared cat could jump to. Lizzie's instinct is to get away from scary sights and sounds, right?"

"Yes. All cats have that instinct," Grandpa Tom said. "They go to the highest spot with the best view. They watch for prey and predators from there."

"There's no way Lizzie would feel safe here," I said. "There's no high place where she can hide or rest or keep watch. That's why she kept leaping to high places at the hotel. She was frightened. Grandpa Tom, could you build a tall cat tree here? One for Lizzie?"

"You bet," he said. "I'd be happy to."

"Great!" I said. "I'll be right back." I leaped off my chair and dashed to the front desk. I asked for Ben.

A minute later, Ben came over. I explained the problem to him, about Lizzie's instinct to climb high to safety.

"So, I won't ever be able to keep her here?" Ben asked sadly.

"No!" I said. "I mean, yes! You can! Grandpa Tom? He built the whole kitty playground at Tabby Towers. He builds great cat trees. And he said he'd build one here! For Lizzie!"

"Okay," Ben said, still looking sad. "But I suppose the tree will have to go in a far, quiet corner, right? I'd really hoped Lizzie could be by the front door, where people would see her. She is the restaurant's namesake."

"But she can be," I said. "The front window would be the perfect place. Cats like sunny spots. They like windows where they can watch birds and squirrels. A quiet corner wouldn't help Lizzie. To feel safest, she needs a perch.

She needs a view of *all* the action – that means people coming and going too. In her mind, they're all predators, because they're larger than she is. Anything smaller than Lizzie seems like prey to her."

Ben's face brightened. "This is *great* news!" he said. "Okay, let's give the cat tree a try.

If it works – if Lizzie keeps her paws off the front desk – you'll have a month of free pizza."

"Trust me, Lizzie will never jump on the front desk again," I promised.

"Tell your grandpa I'll pay for the wood and all the building supplies," Ben said.

"I will. Oh, and another thing," I said. "When Grandpa Tom finishes the tree, don't put Lizzie up there. Let her discover it herself. It will feel safer to her if she believes she's the only one who knows about her hiding spot."

"And don't bother her there. No petting her or anything. If she's left totally alone in her 'secret' place, she'll feel safest."

"Got it. But what if other people touch her?" Ben asked.

"Don't worry, they won't," I said. "Grandpa Tom will make the tree perches very high.

Not even the tallest person will be able to touch Lizzie. He'll make a *No Climbing* sign for kids too."

"Great."

"And you should probably get a shade for the front window," I added. "For super-sunny days. Sphynx can get sunburned easily."

Ben grinned. "I can't thank you enough," he said. "I hope to have Lizzie back here soon."

"You will," I said. "My grandpa's a really fast builder."

I hurried back to the table. A hot slice of pizza waited on a plate for me. Alfreeda and my grandparents were already eating.

I told them the plan, pushed my plate away and asked Grandma Kit for a pen. She dug in her purse and handed me one. I started to draw a cat tree on a paper napkin.

"What is that?" Alfreeda said through a big mouthful of pizza. "No, it can't look like a common cat tree. She's *Queen* Lizzie!"

Alfreeda took the pen from me and started to draw on her napkin. "It has to look like a little kitty castle, high in the clouds," she said.

The pen moved all over the napkin like it had a motor in it. *Wow,* I thought. *Alfreeda's a really good artist.* She made the little cat cave at the top of the tall post look like a real castle. It had towers and a drawbridge. It even had arrow slits.

"She'll have a good view of the restaurant 'forest' from every direction," Alfreeda said, still drawing.

"Queen Lizzie will rule the whole kingdom from high ground," I said. "She'll keep it safe from enemies, like a true queen."

I pointed at the drawing and asked Grandpa Tom, “Can you build that?”

“I can,” he said. “I’ll build a ladder too, so Lizzie can climb up easily. I’ll add a scratching post so she can keep her claws sharp and mark her territory. I’ll hammer the post to the high beam closest to the front door. Lizzie can walk along the beam. That will make her view even wider and her territory even larger.”

“Great!” I said. “Let’s hurry home and start building it!”

“I’ll help,” Alfreeda said.

“Thanks!” I said. And I really meant it.

“Tabitha?” Grandma Kit smiled. “Your pizza. You haven’t eaten one bite.”

“Oh yeah.” I laughed and gobbled two large slices in record time. It was the best-tasting pizza I’d ever eaten – fit for a queen!

I couldn't believe I'd get such tasty pizza *free,* for a whole month!

When Grandma Kit wasn't around, I'd make a secret deal with Alfreeda: If she could go for a whole day without bragging about dogs, I'd share pizza with her that day at dinner time.

Oh yeah, and she wouldn't be allowed to say unkind things about cats for the whole day either. Now *that* would be a purr-fect day at Tabby Towers!

abby
vers

Is a Sphynx the cat for you?

Hello, it's me, Tabitha!

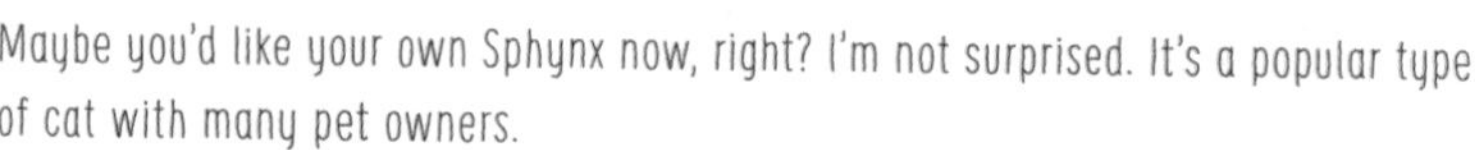

Maybe you'd like your own Sphynx now, right? I'm not surprised. It's a popular type of cat with many pet owners.

Here's why: For one thing, Sphynx look so different from other cats. Many people like strange-looking pets. Second, they're fun to have around. They're smart, friendly and lively. They love getting attention from their families.

But before you buy or adopt one, there are some important things you should know:

Sphynx must be bathed often. The body oil on furry cats spreads to their hair, but the oil on a hairless cat has nowhere to go. So Sphynx must be bathed once or twice a week.

Sphynx can't stand cold weather or too much sunshine. Hairless cats lose more body heat than cats with fur. Sphynx must have warm beds and blankets, in warm areas of the house. In cooler homes or during cold seasons, they may need to wear kitty coats or sweaters to keep them warm enough. Also, owners should limit the amount of sunlight the cats get. Sphynx can get sunburned easily.

Sphynx have a high rate of heart disease. It's important that Sphynx owners plan regular checkups with a vet.

All right, cat lovers! That's all for now . . . until the next adventure at Tabby Towers!

Meowingly yours,

Tabitha Catarina Felinus (Tabby Cat, for short)

Glossary

annoying making someone feel angry or impatient

hairball ball of fur that lodges in a cat's stomach; hairballs are made of fur swallowed by a cat as it grooms itself

health code rule or standard made by the government to protect people's health and safety

instinct behaviour that is natural rather than learned

Middle Ages period of European history from about 500 to 1500

namesake person or thing that has the same name as another

predator animal that hunts other animals for food

prey animal hunted by another animal for food

sprain injury caused by muscle and tissue tearing near a joint

territory area of land that an animal claims as its own to live in

vet doctor who cares for animals

Talk about it

1. Explain why Lizzie's owner wants to check her in at Tabby Towers. What problem is he having with her?
2. Look at the illustration on page 39 and describe what's happening in this part of the story. Make sure you explain the items in the basket and why Tabby is falling down.
3. Step by step, describe Tabby's plan for making Lizzie feel safe at the restaurant.

Write about it

1. Write a five-line poem about Leaping Lizzie. Include descriptive words about how she looks (her skin, ears, paws, etc.) and acts.
2. Write a letter to Ben, the owner of Queen Lizzie's Pizza Palace, that explains what you like, or don't like, about pizza.
3. Write a one-page essay on Sphynx cats. Use at least three sources.

About the author

Shelley Swanson Sateren has been a freelance writer for thirty years and has written more than forty books for children, both fiction and non-fiction. As well as writing, Shelley has worked as a children's book editor and in a children's bookshop. She is also a primary school teacher and has enjoyed employment in several schools. Shelley lives in Minnesota, USA, with her husband and has two grown-up sons.

About the illustrator

Deborah Melmon has worked as an illustrator for more than twenty-five years. After graduating from Academy of Art University in San Francisco, she started her career illustrating covers for the *Palo Alto Weekly* newspaper. Since then, she has produced artwork for more than twenty children's books. Her artwork can also be found on wrapping paper, greeting cards and fabric. Deborah lives in California, USA, and shares her studio with an energetic Airedale Terrier called Mack.

VISIT
TABBY TOWERS
AGAIN WITH
THESE AWESOME
ADVENTURES!

ADVENTURES at
TABBY TOWERS
Leaping Lizzie
Queen Lizzie's Pizza Palace
Illustrated by
Deborah Melmon
Written by
Sateren

ADVENTURES at
TABBY TOWERS
Boxing Bootsie
Written by
Shelley Swanson Sateren
Illustrated by
Deborah Melmon

ADVENTURES at
TABBY TOWERS
Disappearing Darcy
Written by
Shelley Swanson Sateren
Illustrated by
Deborah Melmon

ADVENTURES at
TABBY TOWERS
Fishing Frankie
Written by
Shelley Swanson Sateren
Illustrated by
Deborah Melmon

(WE PROMISED ALFREEDA WE'D INCLUDE THE **HOUND HOTEL** GUESTS AND THEIR SUPER-FUN STORIES HERE TOO!)

www.raintree.co.uk